*Once a she is a t... ... spell-binding prose. Her new collection,* Mirror Image, *is a frightening and yet mesmerizing exercise in base fears and anxieties. Who doesn't dread the morning they get out of bed, look in the mirror and the image not starts speaking to you, but scolds you for your sins? Are you already dead and just don't know it?"*

— Vincent Zandri
*New York Times* and *USA Today* bestselling ITW Thriller and PWA Shamus winning author of *The Remains, The Shroud Key,* and the Dick Moonlight PI Series.

\*\*\*\*\*

*Have you ever lied and cheated to get what you wanted? Then be afraid, very afraid of the mirror that might even follow you to the grave. This mirror knows the truth you've been trying to hide! And if you're the wronged party, be at ease. In Fran Lewis'* Mirror Image *evildoers are held to account. Dancers, actors, students, lawyers, abusers, liars and cheaters can't hide from the truth as author Lewis details cause and effect in chilling detail.*

*After reading this collection of short stories and pondering your own misdeeds, do you still dare face your mirror?* Mirror Image, *by author Fran Lewis is a page-turner.*

— Irma Fritz

\*\*\*\*\*

## 5-STAR READER REVIEWS FOR
# MIRROR IMAGE

*The stories in* Mirror Image *are chilling and every one has a lesson behind it. Beware and be scared!*

— Karen Vaughn, author of *Dead on Arrival*

*****

*Once again Fran Lewis has written a collection of scary stories!* Mirror Image *will keep you up till all hours of the night praying you won't be looking into any mirror where the face looking back isn't yours.*

— Marsha Casper Cook, Michigan Avenue Media

*****

Mirror Image, *a collection of linked short stories by Fran Lewis, delves into our darker side.*
*It's not for the faint of heart!*

—John DeDakis, author of the Lark Chadwick series

*****

# Mirror Image

A COLLECTION OF SHORT STORIES
ABOUT HORRIFIC PEOPLE,
AND THE PRICE THEY PAID FOR THEIR EVIL ACTIONS

FRAN LEWIS

Copyright ©2024, Fran Lewis
ALL RIGHTS RESERVED.

No part of this publication may be reproduced, stored in a retrieval system, or transmitted in any form or by any means—electronic, mechanical, photo-copy, recording, or any other—except for brief quotation in reviews, without the prior permission of the author or publisher.

ISBN: 978-1-962402-87-3

*This is a work of fiction. Unless otherwise indicated, all the names, characters, businesses, places, events and incidents in this book are either the product of the author's imagination or used in a fictitious manner. Any resemblance to actual persons, living or dead, or actual events is purely coincidental.*

# DEDICATION

This dedication took a lot of thought because I realized that I wrote this book to teach a lesson to anyone who does harm to others or who lies. So, I dedicate this book to those who always tell the truth and to the memory of my Dad, David Swerdloff, who taught me honesty, truth and integrity wins out.

And to my first editor for my Faces Behind the Stones series, Maxine Bringenberg. This one is for all you did for me, Maxine. Your words and spirit will shine in my Faces series forever.

—Fran Lewis

# Contents

Mirror Image ............................................................. 1

Miriam's Mirrors ....................................................... 7

The Good Life ......................................................... 12

Welcome to Your Nightmare ................................ 21

The Singer .............................................................. 25

Diminished and Mistreated ................................. 29

A Lawyer with No Morals .................................... 33

Deadly Wrinkle ...................................................... 36

The Wasteland ........................................................ 43

Rumors .................................................................... 48

The mean Teens ..................................................... 54

Toxic Makeup: Beware .......................................... 58

From Beyondthe Grave ........................................ 64

The Plastic Surgeon .............................................. 69

The Killer Pharmacist ........................................... 72

The Actor ................................................................ 76

The Grave Digger ................................................... 81

Bonus Content ....................................................... 89

| | |
|---|---|
| Lies | 91 |
| I Hate Myself | 101 |
| The Con Artists | 109 |
| Going Nowhere | 118 |
| Katie's Untimely Death | 126 |
| Friend or Foe? | 135 |

# INTRODUCTION

This mystical mirror has seen many faces, some innocent and some deserving of punishment. It is the mirror of truth, and it decides the viewer's fate if their life has been spent doing evil.

Following are a collection of stories about some horrific people, the terrible acts they have performed, and the consequences their actions brought upon them. As we all know, there are people in this world who do things so terrible they deserve a punishment just as cruel.

Each person you will meet has done something that warrants the mirror's vengeance. Some will instantly wind up as a face in the mirror, while others will pay a severe penalty before they join those trapped behind the glass. Each time the mirror deals with its intended victim, it moves on to find a new, evil, and deserving person to exact its ultimate judgement upon.

The power that controls the mirror is dangerous, deadly, and just, and no one evil can hide from its truth. Let's move on to meet some of people the mirror targets and what fate awaits them...

# MIRROR IMAGE

What happened to me that fateful morning forever changed my life…

When I looked in my bathroom mirror this morning, I saw someone staring back at me. "Hello, dear," the face said, and I almost passed out.

"Welcome to your new life! I'm the other side of you, the side you really want to show to the world. So, no more being nice, no more being understanding, and no more kind actions. From this point forward, you will be unfeeling, cruel, unrelenting, and vicious as you go after the things you want from life.

"Don't worry that you can't do these things, my dear, I'll be directing everything in your life. I'll make sure you eventually learn to use your evil side to get revenge on the people who deserve your wrath. You *will* follow my rules and do whatever I tell you to do, or someone you love will pay a horrible price.

"Your first task is to put this this Raggedy Ann doll in a sealed box," the voice continued, and suddenly the doll appeared on the cabinet in front of me. "Make sure to wear gloves when you handle it, so your fingerprints aren't on it. Put it in a box and leave it on Mrs. Gold's doorstep.

"Be sure you aren't seen when she opens the door and takes it inside. After she's done that, you will ring the bell again and make sure you're invited in. You will then watch what the doll does and be a witness to the brilliance I created. The revenge it exacts on Mrs. Gold will be truly satisfying. You see, once upon a time, she had a Raggedy Ann doll, and she tortured it relentlessly. She poked its eyes, cut its face, cut holes in it, pulled out its stuffing, and eventually cut off its head, arms, and legs. Now, the doll will do the same to her."

*Mirror Image*

I found I had no control over my body, so I did exactly as the face in the mirror said. When the doll was boxed up, I walked to Mrs. Gold's front door, rang the bell and left quickly so she didn't see me. After Mrs. Gold opened the door and took the box inside, I waited for a few moments, then rang the bell again so she wouldn't connect me with the mysterious box she had just received. She greeted me and showed me to her sitting room where she offered me to sit in a comfortable chair.

After we were both seated, I looked over and saw the box. Knowing that I couldn't leave until she opened it, I asked, "Wow, did someone send you a gift?"

"I don't know," she replied. "The bell rang and when I opened the door, this box was sitting on the front step. There was no card, and I wasn't expecting anything."

"Well, you just have to open it. I love watching people get gifts," I found myself saying.

"Well, okay, dear. Let's see what's inside."

She opened the top of the box and the doll jumped out onto her lap and started talking to her.

"Remember me from your childhood? Remember what you did to me? You tortured me, then you killed me for no reason. Why? I just wanted to be part of your life and bring you joy, but the only thing that seemed to bring you joy was tearing me apart piece by piece. I wanted you to love me like I loved you, but the only love I received in return was pain. Now, it's time for me to give that same love to you."

The doll jumped from her lap, and Mrs. Gold simply stared at it in horror as it began to grow taller. Its grim smile and glowing red eyes terrified her as it bent toward her. "Let's see how you like it when I poke your eyes," it said in a menacing voice as it raised its hand, index finger out, and poked her.

Mrs. Gold screamed, put her hand over her eye, and tried to stand.

"Where do you think you're going? I'm not done showing you my love," the doll said, smiling and showing her its razor-sharp teeth. "How about I tear some holes in you and pull out some of your stuffing? I think that might be fun, don't you?"

"No! Please, don't hurt me. I'm sorry I was so awful to you, but I was a child and didn't know what I was doing."

"Oh, you knew exactly what you were doing, and you enjoyed it. Admit it. It made you feel good to hurt me."

"No! I didn't realize you could feel it. I swear."

"I don't believe you," the doll said. "I think your time for talking is at an end." It grabbed her and held her firmly, then tore out her eyes one at a time with its teeth. When that was done, it ripped her limb from limb until all that was left was a pile of body parts with the gold charm she had been wearing laying on top.

Suddenly, the gory pile on the floor rippled and took on a different shape. When it was done morphing, what was left was a doll with a face that looked just like Mrs. Gold wearing a chilling grin.

I ran out of her house, never looking back. I hoped no one saw me leaving. When I got back inside my house, my heart was racing, but I felt anticipation and excitement for what was next. Horrified, I wondered, *Is my evil side taking over?*

When I passed by the mirror in my entryway, what I saw filled me with dread—Mrs. Gold had joined the original face I'd seen in the mirror. *Would she control my actions and force me to perform a second task?*

# Miriam's Mirrors

Miriam walked into her huge studio where she practiced her dancing for the many shows she hoped to one day star in. Each wall held a different mirror—some that were perfect and added no magnification, and there was one that magnified and made her look overweight. Miriam loved this mirror the most because it made her strive for perfection. She knew she would never be perfect until she looked thin in this mirror.

The worry she felt about her weight magnified, just like her image in the mirror. It had become so bad that when she saw anyone who was even slightly overweight she felt the need to make harsh and brutal comments to them.

*Mirror Image*

---

As her obsession grew, Miriam's behavior became more and more erratic. It had become so bad that the people in her building shied away from her whenever they saw her coming. If they couldn't avoid her, they were treated with rude gestures and taunts about how fat and disgusting they were, regardless of their actual size.

One day, as Miriam gazed into her favorite mirror thinking she had almost reached perfection, something strange happened. The mirror began to glow from within and suddenly spoke. "You are a vane and contemptuous thing who does not deserve this life," the voice said, making her shiver with fear.

When she looked into the mirror again, she wasn't greeted with her almost perfect image. Instead, she saw was a haggard, fat, old woman with gray hair. "No!" she screamed. "If I'm that fat, I won't be able to dance and no one will want me!" Fear and despair overwhelmed her and she covered her eyes with her hands.

"Maybe this isn't real," she said hopefully. "I can't be that horrible woman I saw." When she

*Miriam's Mirrors*

got the courage to peal her fingers from her eyes, she saw her image had returned to normal. She sighed with relief, but it was short-lived.

"If you want to avoid that ugly fate," the scary voice boomed, "you will no longer mock others. If you do not heed my warning, the consequences will be real."

Miriam stood there shaking with fear. "I promise I'll do as you say."

The mirror stopped glowing and was silent.

Miriam was relieved that the voice seemed to have left, and decided she should get to work practicing her dance sequences.

By the time she'd finished her workout, what had happened seemed like a dream. She laughed at herself for being silly, convinced that nothing had really happened.

The next day, she was back to her old self. She berated everyone she came in contact with and enjoyed telling them how disgusting they were.

After a few days, Miriam convinced herself she'd had a small mental breakdown, and the whole episode with the scary voice was just a figment of her imagination. She continued to obsess about her image and weight, and she seemed to increase her bad behavior with anyone unfortunate enough to find themselves in her path. She told herself, "See, nothing bad has happened, so I'm not going to change a thing. I'm so close to perfection, why would I?"

When an entire month had passed, it was clear she was never going to change. On the 31st day after the mirror had spoken, Miriam gazed fondly into it thinking that she'd finally achieved perfection. The glow suddenly infused the mirror again, and the voice said, "Enjoy these last few seconds looking upon your perceived perfection, my dear, for it will soon be gone."

"What do you mean, voice? I can clearly see that I've finally become the size I've always wanted to be."

"Yes, you have, but you ignored my warning and now you're going to suffer the consequences. Never again will you look as you do at this moment. Instead, you'll be obese, clumsy and old."

"No! You can't take it away from me!" Miriam said with horror.

"I can and I will. You had a chance to change and keep your precious looks, but you ignored the warnings I gave you and now you're going to pay the price."

There was a puff of white smoke and when Miriam looked back into the mirror, she was old, severely overweight and gray-headed. "Why would you do this to me?" Miriam cried to the voice.

"I did it because you did not learn your lesson and now you'll never be your idea of perfect again."

Miriam is now the next face in the mirror.

# THE GOOD LIFE

"*It's time for another task,*" the mirror called to those trapped within its web. *Addressing this wrong is long overdue. She has gone far too long without paying for her crimes.*"

The mirror showed them Celine's transgressions as a child, who stole jewelry and money from her parents' store and blamed the thefts on her friends. Some of these children even ended up doing time in juvenile detention.

The scene switched to the day her father became suspicious and then realized his teenage daughter had been the one stealing from him since she was a child and he confronted her. "How can you do this to your friends, and worse to your own parents," Celine's father growled.

*The Good Life*

"We've given you a good life and this is how you repay us?"

"A *good* life?" Celine said with a sneer. "You make me beg and plead for everything I want, so I decided to just take it instead. I deserve way more than you're willing to give to me."

"You are a spoiled and deceitful child, and that's going to change right now," her father vowed.

"We'll just see about that," Celine said, then stormed out of the room.

Later that night, Celine crept into her parents' bedroom and hit each of them over the head with a large rock. Once she was sure they were knocked out cold, she rolled her father off of the bed onto a large, sturdy duvet and then proceeded to drag him to the cellar stairs. It was difficult for her, but she was determined and found the strength. She went down the stairs first, and then dragged her father down, feet first with his head bouncing off each step. When she had him on the cellar floor, she went back for her mother and repeated the process.

When that was done, she wasn't quite sure what to do with them. "I don't think I've got the stomach for outright killing them, but I certainly don't want them interfering in my life anymore. There's no way I'm going to let them keep me from getting everything I deserve."

So, after some careful yet evil thought, she decided to tie them up and leave them in the basement. That way, if she needed something from them, she could still get it…for a while at least. "I wonder how long someone can last without food or water…"

Celine was extremely happy with the way things were turning out. Since she had just turned 18, she quit going to school and started running the store herself. When people asked about her parents, she would sweetly tell them she'd agreed to run the store so they could retire and travel. Everyone praised her for being so selfless and no one really wondered why the couple never returned from their trip.

She liked running the store and keeping all the money for herself, so Celine continued the ruse and started to make a name for herself in the community. She often thought her life was nearly perfect.

*"As you can see, Celine needs to join you,"* the mirror said. *"Miriam, I will give you back your beauty for a time, as long as you convince her you're her friend and make sure vengeance is mine. You will tell her about a huge jewelry show where each store displays their own unique jewelry and the store judged to have the most amazing creation wins $1 million dollars. She's so greedy, she won't be able to pass up this opportunity."*

The Miriam in the mirror rejoined the old, overweight person in this reality and magically transformed to her former young and thin self. She immediately went to Celine's store, where she complimented everything she saw. She laid it on really thick, and Celine ate it up. To help move things along, Miriam bought several pieces, then casually mentioned they should go for coffee sometime.

"You know, I'd really like that," Celine said, realizing she'd become lonely as she'd isolated herself so no one would figure out her gruesome secret. "I'm due for a break, would you like to join me for a treat at the coffee shop down the street?"

"I'd love that," Miriam said, smiling at how easy this was going to be.

The two spent a couple of hours having coffee and scones, and Miriam made sure she stroked Celine's ego the entire time. By the time they were ready to leave, Celine had decided she had a new best friend.

Celine and Miriam got together nearly every day during the next week. They went shopping, had dinner together, and texted each other throughout the day. Celine was thrilled with this new friendship, and she began to let down her guard.

One day while they were having lunch, Miriam pulled a flyer from her purse and showed it to Celine, saying, "This sounds like it was made for you. With all the beautiful things you make

*The Good Life*

for your store, I'm sure you could win the million dollars!"

Celine agreed and couldn't wait to get her hands on all that money. "I think maybe you're right, Miriam," she said as she pulled out her phone. "I'm going to that website right now to fill out the entry form."

Miriam smiled, thinking how easy it had been to manipulate this evil woman.

"There, all done," Celine said with a smug smile. "I guess I'd better get back to the shop and get something made for that show so I can claim my million bucks."

"Oh, I just know you'll win," Miriam said sweetly.

The day of the show, and Miriam picked Celine up to make sure she was right where the mirror wanted her. She wasn't sure what was going to happen, but she hoped she'd be rewarded for doing her part.

When they go there, Miriam noticed that each booth featured a special mirror along with their amazing jewelry creations. She knew what those mirrors meant, so she kept her distance. Celine, however, had no idea and was jealously looking at all the beautiful items that were probably better than what she'd brought. She had been so confident she would win that she hadn't really come up with anything special.

*Well, I'll take care of that,* she thought. *I'll just make sure the best jewelry never gets seen by the judges. I certainly know how to make things disappear. I've been doing it for years,* she thought and chuckled.

"What's so funny?" Miriam asked.

"Oh, nothing. I was just remembering something from my past. Why don't you take a look around while I go register?"

"Sure, that should be fun. I'll see you in a bit."

Celine went to the registration desk, got her table number and went to set up her creations. Once that was done, she took a quick tour of the rest of the entries. She decided a diamond ring and bracelet set were her biggest competition, so she decided to make them disappear. *This is going to be easy, there's not even anyone minding the booth.*

She walked up to the display, acting like she was admiring it, but instead, she quickly snatched the pieces and pocketed them. That being done, she tried to walk away but couldn't. "What's going on?" she said fearfully. "Why can't I move?" Suddenly the ring and bracelet were burning hot, and she quickly flung them out of her pocket.

*"Celine, you've been a very bad girl,"* said a voice that sounded like it was coming from everywhere at once. *"It's time to pay for all the horrible things you've done in your life."*

"I don't know what you're talking about. I haven't done anything," she said indignantly.

*"Oh, I think you have. What about all those times you stole and blamed it on your friends? Then there's the big one, where you imprisoned your parents and starved them to death. I think you've done quite enough, so now it's time for you to take your place with the others in my mirror."*

"What do you mean, 'in the mirror?' I'm not going anywhere."

*"Yes, you are, my dear, and you're going there forever."*

Suddenly, Celine disappeared from view. She'd joined Mrs. Gold and Miriam in the mirror and their tortured reflections showed in the mirrors of every booth at the show.

# Welcome to Your Nightmare

Dee went to bed that night hoping her plans for the day would work out. She was going to skip school with her two friends and go to the mall to hang out. After tossing and turning for hours, Dee decided to get up and make herself some warm milk, hoping that would let her finally get to sleep.

She eventually fell asleep and awoke the next morning not feeling great. She got dressed and headed outside. When she opened the door, the air that hit her in the face smelled putrid. Even though it was 8 a.m., the sun still wasn't up, and it was colder outside than it should be. *What's going on?* she wondered.

Looking around, she saw people wearing masks, acting like they were afraid of the others they saw out walking around. Everything seemed strange and different. *This has to be a dream,* Dee thought as she began wandering aimlessly. The more she walked, the colder she felt.

Suddenly, she heard a hushed and creepy voice say, *"Welcome to your new world, Dee. No one here will care for you or make sure your needs are met. This is a world with no hope. All who live here are looking for meaning, but will never find it. You are here because you chose to ignore all the things good in your life and took the wrong path. In this world, you are alone."*

This new world was unfriendly, and the people were hostile. Just when she'd given up hope, she saw two familiar faces. "Over here!" she shouted to them. "Mom, Dad, it's me, Dee." They ignored her and help walking. "Wait, I want to go with you," she said as she ran toward them. They continued walking like they hadn't heard her, and they disappeared into the crowd of masked faces as she ran closer.

"What am I going to do?" she said with despair. She wandered down the street until she came to a diner. "Maybe I'll know someone in there."

She went in, only to realize this wasn't a diner but instead a funeral home and they were in the middle of a funeral service. As she looked around, she realized everyone there was someone from her past. *I wonder who died,* she thought as she took a seat at the back.

No one noticed her, and she sat all alone. A man in black robes stepped up to the podium and raised his arms above his head and started to chant some fiery words. "This young lady was ungrateful and abusive. She was mean to her pets, fought with her sister and made up lies about a teacher having an affair with the assistant principal. I think we should give her a fitting send off, don't you? Everyone, come on up here. This is your last chance to tell her how you feel about what she did to each of you."

*I've done all of those things he's mentioning,* Dee thought without remorse. *What's going on? Where am I?*

Dee stood with the rest of the crowd and waited her turn to file past the odd coffin with the mirror mounted inside its lid.

She could hear the angry comments each person made as they stood at the coffin, "she was ungrateful," "she was mean," "she bullied everyone," "she took advantage of people," and on and on.

When it was finally her turn at the front of the line, Dee looked down and realized the body in the coffin was hers and one of the faces looking at her from the mirror on the lid was hers as well. She was now in her own personal hell and had joined the faces in the mirror!

# THE SINGER

Ariana was a singer, dancer, and author of a well-known dance instruction book. As she looked into the mirror before her next class, she saw that time was not her friend. She shuddered as she realized her time to shine was running out fast and she'd better do something to guarantee she got her time in the spotlight.

She'd already played that game before to get what she wanted. Even though she had a great voice, she always made sure she came out on top by giving her competition a little "something" in their before-performance drinks. Her little concoction was great for robbing people of their best voices.

Today, the class was practicing for an upcoming TV audition. There was only one lead singer for this one, and Ariana realized that Lola's voice was far superior to hers. It was time to make another special drink.

Lola was eliminated due to a hoarse voice and troubled breathing. She eventually wound up in the ER, but they could not figure out what caused the problem.

Ariana was positive this would mean she got the lead, but the director brought in another singer instead, and she was furious.

*How am I going to deal with her?* Ariana wondered. *There's no way I'm going to let her take this part—it's mine! They used my book to set up these tryouts, so I know how this works. If she can't dance, then she won't get the part. I'll just have to make sure she can't dance.*

The mirror was watching and listening and knew it was time to teach Ariana a lesson she would never forget.

When it came time for the other singer to dance, Ariana had already put her plan in place. She'd applied Vaseline to various areas on the stage so the other singer would slip as she danced.

*The Singer*

Ariana danced first, and avoided the traps. The applause was great when she'd finished, almost guaranteeing her success.

When the other girl took to the stage, the first leap she attempted caused her to slip on a Vaseline-covered spot. She twisted and landed in a heap on the stage, breaking her right leg and her wrist. Ariana ran over to her and told her not to move as she called 911, while secretly gloating about how well her plan had worked.

The mirror was certain now, and Ariana had just sealed her fate. It was time to find just the right person to sabotage her reputation and relationships and teach her a lesson.

Since Ariana enjoyed cheating some of her students by charging them double for their classes, the mirror thought this would be the way to trap her. Once one of her clients decided to spread the word about her fleecing them, things would start to crumble.

The face in the mirror enlisted the thoughts a girl named Asia, who was just a kid who just wanted to get off the streets and make it as a dancer. Poor Asia never knew what hit her, as the mirror manipulated her to sabotage Ariana by replacing the music for her audition. Instead of the intended music, scary voices and messages filled played and she looked like a fool as she tried to fake it and pretend this was her intended piece.

The result was Ariana no longer was a contender for the lead part and her reputation was ruined and no one in the business would even consider her for anything else. The mirror was satisfied and Ariana became just another face captured by its traps.

# Diminished and Mistreated

Bosco despised his wife, Beatrice. As her dementia grew worse, Bosco blamed her for everything going wrong in his life, claiming she was holding him back from greatness. He felt sorry for himself, so he constantly neglected and berated Beatrice.

One day when he stepped into the bathroom to take a shower, he heard a voice coming from the mirror. When he looked up, an altered version of his face was staring back at him.

"You are cruel to her," it said. "You don't feed her well or take care of her. You leave the door open with deranged hopes of her wandering away. You will suffer and find out exactly what it's like when no one cares about you."

My mother, a neighbor to Bosco and Beatrice, did not know the extent of the situation further than Beatrice's daily presence at my mother's apartment. Each morning, once Beatrice is dressed, Bosco shows her to the door, genuinely hoping she would wander away so she no longer has to be his problem. Beatrice disappeared one day, and he felt a sense of relief.

As my mother and I were headed to the store we saw Beatrice walking alone, and we were afraid she was going to get hurt. I quickly jumped out of the car to bring Beatrice to safety. When we reached her apartment, Beatrice told us she was afraid of the place, yet she did not seem to know why.

Her husband was visibly angry once he saw who was on the other side of the door, and he glared at us, then took Beatrice roughly by the arm into the apartment.

Bosco soon realized that he could not force her away, so he hired a young girl to watch over her at all times since he refused to care for her. Beatrice occasionally came up to my mother's apartment still. She told my mother how said she felt, still not knowing the exact reason for her depressive state.

A few days later my mother heard an ambulance come, she saw them take Beatrice away and rush to the hospital. Soon after, we found out Beatrice had died.

Her husband looked as if he was relieved, and he did not show a speck of sadness whatsoever. He refused to help out with the funeral and left all worries behind him with his wife. Her funeral was small, and Bosco did not show.

The day after the funeral, Bosco came home and headed to the bathroom. As he glanced at himself in the mirror, he recognized the face of Beatrice looking back at him. He was shocked, unable to move. Beatrice smiled down at him with a sinister sneer and snarled, "If you think you've won, think again."

His body lifted into the air and suddenly he was inside the mirror, lonely and surrounded by the dark. Beatrice looked at him from outside the mirror, smiled and said, "I am free now! I am free, and you will pay for your sins."

Beatrice got the final laugh.

# A LAWYER WITH NO MORALS

She has taken advantage of her clients, family, friends, and whoever else she could get her hands on. Thinking of other people? Selflessness? Neither exist when it comes to her. As a person in the legal profession, her role is to defend and protect, yet her concern is what she can take from each person in an already vulnerable situation. She steals money and forges signatures for personal endeavors. She speaks in lies and threats when her desires are not fulfilled.

A woman, a lawyer, of no morals and only selfish desires looks into the mirror. She sees the reflection of her face in the mirror but along with scars, cuts and bruises on other parts of her body which she has never seen before.

There is a voice speaking from inside the mirror to her. It says,

"This is who you really are: destructive, cruel, heartless, and remorseless. There is a mark on your body for each person you have hurt throughout your life. You lie, steal, and create false statements throughout your work. You will pay, and it will be when you least expect it."

Faces of others who have sinned appear in the mirror and the voice speaks to her once more,

"The faces within the mirror are people who have been punished for their cruel actions. If your treacherous actions are not brought to an end, you will join them."

The lawyer looked at each face in the mirror and saw how pained and miserable every single one of them looked. This changed her life and she decided that this was not what she wanted for her life.

She was one of few people who changed for the better and avoided a terrible fate. The mirror was satisfied and moved on to its next victim.

# Deadly Wrinkle

Erna is a specialist in creating beauty products for the upper-class woman. She uses ingredients she claims no person is allergic to. Yet, she isn't really sure this claim is true.

Because of this small doubt, she requires that each of her clients sign an agreement stating they won't hold her responsible if they have problems with her products.

Wrinkle creams are the most popular of her wares among women age 40 and older. They all hope the treatments will make their wrinkles disappear like magic, leaving them with smooth, young-looking skin.

Bertha, a 55-year-old wealthy woman, has wrinkle-free skin, except for one area on her chin. So, she went to Erna asking for a full treatment. Erna feels like Bertha is speaking down to her, so she decides to teach her a lesson. She mixes a "special" treatment just for Bertha, and includes ingredients she's sure will cause an allergic reaction.

Erna applies the cream all over Bertha's face, even though the area on her chin is the only concern. On the first application of the cream, Bertha's skin feels fine, better even. Yet, on the second application, Bertha's skin becomes itchy and irritated. Erna tells her it's a part of the treatment, and to trust the process.

Hives and rashes appear all over Bertha's face, and then her skin starts peeling. What's worse is she's also struggling to breathe. Erna acts concerned and calls an ambulance right away, as if she wasn't the one who caused this to happen.

Once at the emergency room, the doctors are baffled by what they are seeing on Bertha's face. The top layer of skin on her face is almost completely disintegrated.

The doctors check her blood and take samples from her face. When the tests come back, they show arsenic, Isopropyl acetone, methyl ethyl ketone, n-methyl-pyrrolidone and other toxic substances that all have a drying or burning effect when applied to the skin.

When confronted about this by Bertha, Erna says this can't be from her products. Bertha is suspicious and Erna acts offended. Bertha eventually recovers and steers clear of Erna and her products from then on.

Erna, of course, doesn't care. Just to be safe and get away from the rumors about her products, she moves her business to a new location and changes the name to Wrinkle No More. She also changes her name to Ina.

All is going well with the new business and Ina has many new clients. One day, Tonya comes into the salon, and Ina decides she is too vain and obnoxious to deserve her wonderful products. Instead, she works her magic and gives Tonya a "special" session, telling her she's receiving it because she's a first-time client.

Tonya is thrilled to get special treatment, so she lays down on the table and is ready to be transformed. She feels kind of odd after the cream is applied to her face, but she puts her trust in Ina because she's heard good things from others who use her products.

After the application of the moisturizer, Tonya's face begins to itch and her skin feels like it is flaking off. Horrified, she demands a mirror to see what's happening. Ina tells her this is a natural reaction and refuses to give her a mirror.

Tonya doesn't believe this, and takes out her compact to look at her face. What she sees is that the top layer of her skin is, in fact, peeling off.

She freaks out and screams at Ina, "*What did you do to me!*"

Ina calmly responds, "You've always been the prettiest girl. In high school you used to make fun of me and the other girls because we couldn't afford fancy makeup like you. You were terrible to everyone around you. So, now your skin will never be the same, and you'll never be the best-looking girl around ever again!"

Tonya is furious and storms out of Ina's business. She decides revenge is the only way to deal with Ina. Tonya's plan is to go into the store like she is buying groceries, so it does not seem like she's doing anything suspicious. She grabs spices, several types of rat poison and insect killers, liquid soap, cola, ginger ale, along with the rest of her normal groceries.

While she's shopping, Tonya runs into Ina's assistant, Pat. "Wow, are you having some sort of issue, Tonya's?" Pat asks after noticing the copious amounts of poisons in Tonya's shopping cart.

"Why, yes, I've had an infestation of rats and roaches at my house recently. It's just horrible!"

"Oh, I'm sorry to hear that. I hope you get that taken care of," Pat says as she walks away to do her own shopping.

Once Tonya arrives home, she begins to concoct a horrific formula. When it's finished, it even melts the faces off the dolls she uses as test subjects. *Now, how am I going to get Ina to put this on her face without me getting blamed for what it does to her,* Tonya wonders. *Maybe that innocent little Pat could convince her to use it? Hmm, that might just work.*

The next day, Tonya invites Pat to a local café and shows her the new cream she's invented. She tells Pat it will make the customers at the salon look really young and wrinkle-free. "Why, this magic cream even fixed all the problems I was having with my skin," she tells Pat. "Do you think Ina would consider selling this at her salon? I'd be willing to give her a free sample so she can try it first to make sure it works."

"Well, I suppose I could ask," Pat said with hesitation. There was something odd about how eager Tonya was to get Ina to try her concoction.

"Thank you so much. You don't know how happy that makes me," Tonya said, handing over the jar of cream.

Pat was true to her word and gave the cream to Ina when she went into work later that day. Ina, being greedy as always, could only imagine how much she could make from this cream. There wasn't all that much in the jar, so she decided she wouldn't use it on herself she'd just sell it directly to her clients at a huge price.

The next day, all of the clients in her store were eager to try the new cream and handed over their payments with smiles on their faces. That didn't last long though. Once the cream was applied to their faces, their skin began to burn and peal. Everyone was screaming, "My face feels like it's melting off!" and "Get it off me!" and "Oh, God, the pain is unbearable!" and on and on.

Ina couldn't believe it. In the span of a few minutes, her reputation was ruined. Her former clients were furious and had banded together to sue her for everything she had.

Feeling sorry for herself, she looked in the mirror. She was shocked to see the face smiling back wasn't hers. Then, the face spoke, saying, "You enjoy hurting others, and have done so repeatedly with no remorse. Because of that, I judge you and sentence you to be trapped in this mirror for eternity."

The mirror had claimed another face.

# THE WASTELAND

Mothers are supposed to protect their children and provide everything they need in life, both emotionally and physically. This is not the case for Ingrid, who is the most horrific mother in every way possible.

Ingrid's children fear her and continually pray she will disappear, die or simply just go away. They are miserable and feel like any life would be better than the one they have.

Her two daughters aren't allowed to wear decent-looking clothes. Their mother dresses them in the worst clothing she can find at second-hand stores.

So, each day the girls leave the house early to go to their friend's house to change into better clothes their friend has lent to them. They made their friend promise to never tell anyone what they're doing.

One morning, the girls continue their usual routine. Today, though, Ingrid leaves the house right after them to run some errands. As she gets ready to go inside a store across from the school, she notices her girls wearing different clothing.

Ingrid doesn't say anything about this to the girls when they get home from school. In the morning, however, the girls wake up to find all of their clothes are gone. All they have to wear are the pajamas they slept in, and Ingrid angrily dares them to borrow clothes from their friend again.

The girls walked to their friend's house in their pajamas, with no coats, socks or shoes. "How can our mother be so cruel?" their friend's mother asked when she opened the door and saw them standing there. "Doesn't she care even a little what happens to you? Let's get you some clothes, coats and shoes so you can get to school."

Once the children left, the mother called Child Protective Services and reported the extremely harsh way Ingrid was treating her children. The CPS representative, who was also an agent for the voice in the mirror, was angered by the story she heard and the repercussions for Ingrid were harsh.

Ingrid's punishment was to stay in a place to be feared — The Wasteland. In this place, the oxygen is thin, and storms and fires have destroyed nearly everything. It is a world of deserts, sandstorms, scalding sun, and little drinkable water. There are only burnt down neighborhoods perfumed with the strong stench of a multitude of dead animals. Only the cruelest of people are exiled to this world. There is no hope and no escape.

Ingrid was transported to this barren world with nothing but what she was wearing, just as she'd done to her poor children. She now knows what it feels to truly have nothing. Rather than being sorry for the behavior that brought her here, her only thoughts are how she can punish her children for putting her through this.

As she looks around this world, she wonders, *How am I supposed to survive here?* Starting a fire becomes her first priority, because it's freezing cold. After rubbing two sticks together for a very long time, she eventually creates a fire. She finds a large tin can and scoops the fire into it, feeding it so it will keep burning for a while.

Now that the fire's mobile, Ingrid wanders around until she finds a house that will offer a little shelter. Everything inside is filthy and old. Brown water trickles from the faucet, and no matter how long she lets it run it will never be clean enough to drink.

Going into a bedroom, Ingrid finds a large, rustic mirror. She looks into it and sees herself, wondering, *What did I do to deserve being dumped into this disgusting place? Is it to test my survival skills?*

As she continues to look into the mirror, a voice that sounds like it's coming directly out of the mirror says, "Ingrid, you are here for a reason. You hurt those around you and feel no remorse. Here, you will receive exactly what you deserve."

*The Wasteland*

Suddenly, Ingrid is surrounded by the specters of the people she's terrorized throughout her life. Each of them takes a turn yelling at her. Her daughters, the school principal, the people in the market who witnessed her berating and beating her girls in public, and so many more.

None of their words fazed her, so the specters switch to taking turns hitting her. Their hands leave marks on her skin and rip her clothes. Eventually, she left standing there in just her slippers.

Ingrid, still unrepentant even stripped of everything, becomes another face trapped forever in the mirror.

# RUMORS

Zena loves to gossip about her friends, and does so relentlessly. She feels no guilt when the gossip hurts others, in fact, she enjoys that.

When she looks in the mirror this morning, she's shocked by what she sees. As she whimpers and touches her ruined face, the mirror says, "Evil brings evil, and spreading lies will only get you something you don't want. Think before you speak, or you will be trapped forever just like the rest of us."

When the voice finishes speaking, Zena's reflection goes back to normal and she decides that maybe she's stressed out and seeing things. So, she goes about her day without thinking twice about what the voice told her.

## Rumors

Zena has always been jealous of Nona, who lives in a big house with workout room in the basement that boasts a music system a huge wide screen TV. Zena has none of these things in her home. Nona also has closets filled with designer clothing and shoes, while Zena has a limited wardrobe and none of it has designer labels. Zena would do anything to change places with Nona.

So, she devises a wicked plan to make that happen. She's great at forging documents, and faking things like videos. She even has a side hustle where she creates fake IDs to earn extra money and forges report cards for kids at her school.

Zena and Nona both struggle in school — Zena, because she doesn't try, and Nona because studying is difficult for her. Zena loves that oh-so-popular Nona isn't perfect at everything, and she plans to capitalize on that.

Zena's master scheme is to spread rumors about Nona to ruin her reputation so she won't be popular anymore. She plans to fake a video of Nona stealing test answers from Mr. Jon's cabinet that he always keeps unlocked because he trusts his students.

Zena pays another student that looks like Nona from behind to steal the test. Then, on test day, she taped the test answers under Nona's desk before everyone got to class. It's no secret that Nona struggles to get good grades. So, when Zena happened to mention to the teacher that she saw something under Nona's desk, it wasn't that difficult for him and everyone else to believe Nona was planning to cheat.

After people began talking about Nona getting caught, Zena decided to make things even worse and began telling people Nona was sleeping with Mr. Jon and that's how she got the test. While these rumors spread, Zena anonymously sent the video of "Nona" taking the test answers to Mr. Jon.

Mr. Jon quickly contacted the principal about the video and the next day, Nona was accused of not only planning to cheat but also stealing test answers. Nona denied everything, and because

*Rumors*

she'd never done anything like this before the principal only gave her a two-day suspension.

Zena was furious when she found out Nona's punishment was so small. So, she decided to up her game and went to the bad part of town to buy some drugs. Once she had them, she planted them in Nona's locker.

The next day, Zena used the rumor mill to spread accusations that Nona used drugs. Her rumor network was effective, and soon the principal knew about it too. He called the police and they brought their drug-sniffing dogs and went to check Nona's locker after receiving an anonymous tip courtesy of Zena.

When they opened the locker, there were multiple drugs inside. Nona was terrified and shaken to the core by what they found, but she'd felt weird all day and couldn't seem to focus long enough to defend herself from the accusations. She was immediately sent to get her blood tested and then taken to a holding cell at the jail.

When her blood test came back, she was indeed under the influence. Nona had no idea how this could be, but she did feel extremely ill. She couldn't think clearly, so she laid down on the cot in her cell and closed her eyes for a while.

Zena went home from school that day feeling extremely accomplished. Her plan had worked like a charm and popular Nona was the school darling no more.

When she went into the bathroom to wash up for dinner, the mirror came alive and gave her a dire warning. Refusing to believe this was real, she shook her head, turned off the light and left the room.

As she came downstairs, there was a knock at the front door. When she opened the door, it was the police. "We're here to ask you about the drugs we found in your friend Nona's locker earlier today," the officer said.

"I don't know anything about that," Zena said angrily. "Besides, she deserves whatever her consequences she gets because she thinks she's better than everyone! I don't know what you want from me."

"You deny any knowledge of the drugs found in her locker?" the officer asked.

"Of course. Why would I know anything about that?"

"Fine, but I'll be back if I find anything that connects you to this."

"I don't know why you're even here," Zena said, slamming the door as the officer turned and walked away.

*"If you don't repent your horrific actions, you'll be trapped in my mirror for eternity,"* a voice said in Zena's head.

Zena ran into the bathroom and yelled at the mirror, "You wouldn't dare! "

"Oh, but that's where you're wrong," the voice said, as Zena became the next face in the mirror.

# THE MEAN TEENS

Some teens feel the need to go out and drink with their friends without thinking of the consequence their actions — they just want to be in the moment. Two 17-year-olds, Jena and Dina, both just got their driver's licenses, so they've decided to go out with friends to celebrate by drinking.

When Jena was getting ready, she looked at her face in her bedroom mirror and saw something that startled her. Her face had cuts and bruises, her nose looked broken, and her lips were severely swollen. Then she heard a voice that said, "Be careful or this is how you'll end up if you drink and drive." Of course, she thought this was just her imagination and didn't change her plans.

*The Mean Teens*

Jena picked up all of her friends, and they decided they wanted to make one more stop to pick up a girl they all liked to torment. When they got there, Jena went to the door and when Trina answered, she asked, "Hey, would you like to come have a drink with us? We're just going back to my house."

Trina was surprised by the invitation and quickly grabbed her coat, yelling to her mother that she was going out with friends for a while.

She quietly scooted into the back seat of Jena's car, thinking, *I've never had alcohol before, but it's nice to finally be included.*

Since the mean girls knew Trina probably wouldn't be too willing to drink, they decided they'd take care of that for her. When they got to Jena's house, Trina got a soda from the refrigerator, deciding alcohol wasn't a good idea.

When she left to go to the bathroom, the other girls carefully poured vodka into her soda and swirled it around to mix it.

Tina came back and took a long drink of her soda, puzzled by how bad it tasted. After a few more sips, though, she didn't notice the taste anymore. By the time everyone was ready to leave, Trina had finished her soda and was feeling dizzy and a little sick. The girls even laughed at her as she wobbled drunkenly around the room looking for her coat.

They decided Dina would drive everyone home, since she seemed the least drunk. Unfortunately, Dina lost control of the car, hit another car, and their vehicle ended up smashed into a tree. When Dina looked into the backseat, she saw Trina's neck was broken and she looked day, while Jena was breathing but badly injured.

The other girls saw this too, and since they were unhurt, they fled the scene quickly. Dina was left not knowing what to do, so she decided to get out of the car and walk home like she'd never been there.

When she got home, Dina went to the bathroom to see if any of her injuries were obvious. She looked into the mirror, and a voice boomed, "You will pay for what you did, Dina, and you will relive this night for eternity as you're trapped in the mirror!"

Dina was now just another face trapped in the mirror.

# Toxic Makeup: Beware

The air turns black around her as icy fingers grip her arms in the darkness. The bleak surroundings give her chills, and the unspoken words and demonic stare put fear in her heart as she falls to the hard ground. Inside a dismal house with just a bed and a filthy blanket, she realizes that someone is there, but she can't see who.

A raspy sounding voice comes from an odd source.

"Your stay here will be permanent, and there is no escape unless you repent, change your evil ways, and fix the horrific things you have done to so many. Do you see the small mirror on the wall? Each day, it will show you the mirror images of what is left of so many people you have destroyed. You have no way out, and your fate will be decided by your actions and words."

She feels icy fingers around her legs and sees a vision in the mirror that turns her face red.

"You hurt so many with your toxic beauty products. Your clients constantly end up in the Emergency Room because of the harmful chemicals you sneak into your products. You will learn what happens when you endure the same beauty treatments and the same toxins unless you undo your damage and find a way to fix the faces of those that have been disfigured and ruined. You will become all of those stricken faces in your mirror if you do not repent."

S is her name, and she has no remorse for what she has done. Money is her goal, and her primary targets are rich and beautiful women looking to be models or flaunt their perfection. S is not the most attractive person. She has a big nose, wide forehead, and lips the size of a cow. She is anything but pretty, and her makeup choices are overpowering and make her face look like a clown.

*Mirror Image*

When she looks in the mirror and sees her reflection, she is given a warning that what she now sees will be what will happen to her if she keeps on using toxic products. She blows this off, laughing at her reflection, and continues on with opening her shop. The face in the mirror is a blur in her mind, no longer a part of her thoughts.

Clearing her mind, she welcomes her first client and places the products on her tray next to her chair. First, she uses the moisturizer, then she chooses a base, a color not too dark nor too light. The lip gloss she picks is pink and sparkly, along with a light brown contour and a concealer under the eyes to hide the dark spots.

Everything seems fine until the client's face begins to itch, her eyes water, and her lips swell. The smile on S's face tells the client exactly what has been done. S purposely destroyed her client's face, killing every chance of her being able to enter the beauty pageant. S even goes to the extent of telling her client that she will never be able to even walk through the door or sign up as a contestant. The client flies out of her chair to go to the ER, but nothing can repair the damage. The doctors are able to remove the poisons safely, but the damage will forever remain.

This is just the beginning of S's day, and now that she cleaned up after the first client, she is waiting for a famous model to enter, hoping to create a new look for her as well. This client also wants body makeup. S plans to do more damage on this model than on her first client, but since a woman is there to watch S as she works on the model, she changes her method up a little bit. S first puts a base of moisturizer with no toxins to prevent the burning from happening immediately. Moving on to the harmful products which S added more ingredients to, S hopes it will not only irritate her skin but also burn it to the point her skin peels off.

As S planned, the model does not feel the full impact of the makeup until she washes up in the shower after a full day of work. The model rubs soap all over her body, inadvertently rubbing the toxic makeup into her skin. She passes out from the pain of the burning and the sight of rashes and chunks of her skin in her hands.

To call S's shop is pointless because she disconnected her phone lines, closed her business down, and reopened a few towns over.

When opening her new beauty salon and scheduling clients, she decides to not use any of her toxic materials unless someone deserves it. Yet, that does not last long because her first client is demanding, overbearing, and critical of S's appearance. She decides not only to irritate this client's skin but also to torture her.

Going back to her supply room, S grabs soaps and cleaning products used on floors. She mixes all she can into some of her normal products. Applying these products onto her client's skin brought a smug smile to her face. Her client's face turns red from the products and from her excruciating screaming. S does not stop here, she continues to pat alcohol into her client's skin, telling her that this feeling is completely normal.

The client does not believe her, so she jumps out of the chair and pries her eyes open to look into the mirror to see if the damage looks as bad as it feels. The client curses at S while she quickly leaves the boutique.

Smiling at what she has done, S does not see the mirror and the face that is looking back at her. She carries on happily, checking her own makeup. She uses clean products to treat her own skin, but she does not realize that the toxic one happened to get mixed in. Looking at her face in the mirror, she sees a deadly smile staring back at her, something that will change her forever.

The face in the mirror is a mixture of the faces of all the clients she has caused damage to. This face is now hers.

The mirror tells her, "I warned you. You did not repent and change your ways, so here is your new look. This is what you are now since your jealousy and ego have become too much."

Now another face in the mirror, she is stuck as a representation of all the damage she has caused.

# From Beyond the Grave

Some people never get justice during their lifetime, and there is a dead man who journaled throughout his life and requested in his will that his story be shared. He is a dead man wanting to clarify his "sins." With much time on his hands in prison, he wrote about this certain situation in his life.

Dr. Goldenberg is a renowned surgeon, and Fiona is the woman who put him in situations which he did not deserve: a courtroom, prison, and absolute helplessness.

"Fiona came into my office after realizing her serious medical issues could not get fixed by her doctor which she has been going to for 15 years.

My nurse gave her a regular checkup by recording her basic information and taking films of some problematic areas, so I then follow up by telling Fiona the issues that we have found: a cyst deep in her left arm and a suspicious cyst in her jaw.

"I repeatedly told Fiona that even though she cannot see or feel these cysts, that doesn't mean that they are not problematic. I told her that we would like to take some more x-rays, but she refused my concern.

"She had then gone to one of my fellow colleagues, Dr. Hans, claiming that I had not given her proper treatment, nor had I notified her about what I had found. I told Dr. Hans about her case, what I had found, and what I propose as a treatment for her. Dr. Hans never contacted me again after that, which I thought was odd.

"After a while, I chose to forget about my weird encounter with Fiona and how Dr. Hans seemed to overlook my advice. That was until a court date showed up on my front porch one morning demanding that I be there with a lawyer.

"I constantly thought to myself, *What had I done wrong?* Yet, I could not think of a single thing. I have only helped and healed all throughout my life!

"I showed up to my court date promptly with my lawyer and found that Dr. Hans was with Fiona. *What in the world!* I had thought. I was incredibly dumbfounded with the situation I was in. 'Why am I here?' I asked their direction. The only response I got was from Fiona saying, 'You'll find out.'

"Throughout our time in court Fiona had brought up many scans by Dr. Hans, claiming that I had these same scans yet held the information from her. She even brought up the fact that I am one of the best surgeons and with that title comes helping and healing people. She completely disregarded our conversation where I proposed a plan of action to treat her cysts. It seemed as though Fiona had a personal vendetta against me, and when I looked over at Dr. Hans, who was my colleague and my friend, he had a victorious smirk across his face. He loved every minute of this because throughout our lives I had always been better at what we do, so he was radiating joy by seeing me in that vulnerable position. Even my legal team did nothing to support me. I had never felt so helpless before.

"At the end of the case, I had been backstabbed my legal team, my patient, and my closest colleague. There was nothing I could have done or said that would have made anyone hear me. Yet, I found myself yelling, 'I have a family! You are wrongfully imprisoning a man with a family and man who saves lives! She refused my help!'

"It was useless to even try. I was taken away in hand cuffs, accused of withholding information that was crucial to a patient's wellbeing.

"I wrote my story because I am not the villain that I was set out to be. I chose to help Fiona while she chose to perpetrate her anger from other people in the world onto me. I chose to keep silent in hope that someone would stand up for me until I realized I am the only one who can advocate for me. Even though I will be dead soon, and my time is as good as gone, I am here now to say shake off those who don't believe in you, take on those who stand in your way, and continue to live unbounded and as free as you can.

"Although I have lived my life in a prison cell, I have accepted what has happened, yet I have never found true peace in that situation nor inside this small, barred room."

The mirror had taken Dr. Goldenberg's legal team, Dr. Hans, and Fiona as faces in the mirror, yet Dr. Goldenberg was left in a prison cell the rest of his life. Although they were penalized for their actions, he never received peace because of what they had done.

# The Plastic Surgeon

Marvin prides himself on the fact that he is one of the ugliest men on the face of the planet. He is the creator of his features; his nose, lips, and ears were all formed in odd ways by himself. Marvin has this skill of making people as beautiful or ugly as he wants them. He is a plastic surgeon who hates men and women who are vain, but despises those who become fond of his assistant, Dina. He is very protective when it comes to her.

Fred Miller, Marvin's first client on a cold December morning, comes in to have his nose and ears made smaller. Marvin examines Fred from head to toe to check his health and he notices that Fred is checking out Dina at the same time. Marin's protective side comes in, and he tells Fred that he will not only fix his ears and nose but also remove the mole on his shoulder. Fred was extremely thrilled about this kind gesture.

Marvin's plan is to make Fred uglier than he. A few bumps in his nose and elf ears? Absolutely. Deform Fred's shoulder so his head permanently tilts to the side? Heck yeah!

As Marvin washes his hands, he looks into the mirror to see his reflection. His features all deformed but it doesn't matter because Dina doesn't treat him differently because of them. He loves Dina, and he should be the only person to ever be able to look at her. She is his.

Suddenly, his features become fixed and "normal." The mirror speaks to him, "If you were not deformed, then would you have this possessiveness over Dina? She may have liked you before, but she is even fonder of you now because of your uniqueness. She is a kind woman, and anyone can see that, even Fred. He needs love, too. Don't let your possessiveness control you, or you will deeply regret it. I will make you regret it."

Marvin laughs at the mirror, "There is not anything you could possibly do."

He goes into the surgery room and deforms Fred's nose, ears, and takes a large chunk out of his shoulder.

Right after the surgery, Marvin proudly heads to another room to clean himself up and change out of his scrubs. The mirror in the corner speaks to him. "I warned you, Marvin. I warned you and since you did not listen, you will rue the consequences!"

He fears leaving Dina, and he becomes another face in the mirror living the rest of his life watching Dina fall in love with Fred.

# The Killer Pharmacist

Pharmacist are very powerful people. They can dispense drugs of all kinds to unsuspecting people who are just hoping to be cured. A pharmacist in Florida has his home filled with a multitude of medications which he has doctored up for special circumstances that require killing his patients.

Inside his soundproof basement, he has a special fireplace where he burns his victims yet, on certain occasions, he will sell the bodies to medical schools. His favorite victims are trusting college students and teens who are searching for any kind of drug that will make them high.

The pharmacist, Dr. Jones, is a dangerous man. He is a well-fashioned, rich, and desirable man and he knows it. He often will check himself out in his bedroom mirror and even talk to his image.

Mary Jane is his first victim for the month. She comes to him needing a refill on her prescribed Vicodin. Dr. Jones gives her a medication which looks similar to Vicodin, and since she has been out of the medication for a few days, she takes it right away. All of a sudden, she becomes very affectionate, flirtatious, and very shaky with her actions and in her voice. She left his office, hardly being able to make it home.

Later on, she goes to the bank to withdraw money, yet she they tell her that her account will no longer service her because it now belongs to Dr. Jones.

Little did Mary Jane know, the disclaimer which she signed before receiving her refill was actually a release of all of her money, life insurance, and her car to Dr. Jones. When signing that paper, she completely trusted him that it was just a disclaimer of any adverse symptoms she may have.

She quickly goes to Dr. Jones' office in hope to clear this situation up, yet she finds the office doors locked. She then heads to his apartment, and there is no response when she knocks on the door, so she decides to just go in. After she enters the apartment, Dr. Jones comes out of hiding and inject a huge amount of hypodermic needle into her arm.

Her face turns red, her body shakes, and he looks into the closest mirror to see himself so demonic that it makes him laugh.

Over the course of the next few days, Dr. Jones sees several more patients wanting their prescriptions filled. Like Mary Jane, he has each one of them sign the "disclaimer" and they all end up with a needle in their arm and all of their belongings signed over to him. The images of himself in the mirror all have the same dangerous smile until the final patient.

"Dr. Jones, you have taken over 20 lives of young people for greed, malicious intent, and experimentation of new drugs you created. You stare at yourself in the mirror as if you are the smartest and most handsome man in the world, yet you are just an evil man who overlooks the importance of the innocent and vulnerable young people you have killed. What about their families? You are a walking weapon, only caring about the money you receive from this. Do you have any feelings of remorse?"

The look on his face is more demonic that that of any known serial killer. His face becomes a combination of each of his victims when he looks into the mirror.

"Dr. Jones, since you will not repent and try to undo your damage, you will now take my place in this distorted mirror which now holds your new image and your destiny."

# The Actor

The mirror does not lie, only I do. The mirror changes each time I look at myself, knowing that eventually the images that I see will all blend into one horrific sight.

Lying, cheating, and maiming anyone that gets in my way has never bothered me at all, but this one last deed might take everything I have ever earned, legally or not, away. It is my last chance at fame on the silver screen, and there is no way I will let anyone get the part I deserve. They will live to regret it because there are no limits to what I may do.

The mirror warns me when I see my reflection, "If you continue in this way, trying to destroy other people for the part, you will pay dearly, and you will be another face in a huge mirror that everyone will see every day."

The voice in the mirror fades from my mind and memory as I come into the studio and auditions beginning.

I am going in to read the lead part in Macbeth and another part in Julius Caesar. Those who audition for one of the roles will be a lead actor in both Macbeth and Julius Caesar. While auditioning, my voice comes out a little strained, yet some other actors that I listen to on the other side of auditioning room door are more forceful and confident when acting. Realizing that I probably will not get the part, I grow angry and vengeful.

When the director comes out of the auditioning room, he tells me the part is not mine, so I demand that I read the part again. I refuse to give up this opportunity, so I throw lies, threats, and photos of him with the leading lady playing Lady Macbeth at him. He will be more than screwed if his wife gets a hold of those photos since she owns the studio.

The color washes from his face, but he holds true to his decision of the leading actor, saying that he is better for both plays.

I leave the studio with the photos to decide what my next move is going to be. If my plan goes right, then the handsome, rugged, and perfect leading actor will no longer be so capable of taking on this job, let alone breathing.

I catch up with the new leading actor and ask to celebrate with him. I tell him that I am a supporting actor, and I would like to get to know him since we are going to be together on set quite a bit.

The man agrees, so we head to the closest bar. Since we are shooting the next day, we choose nonalcoholic drinks, Ginger Ale and Club Soda. We start off with some small talk, but soon he leaves to use the restroom. I take this as my chance to sneak some colorless poison, hydrochloric acid and ethylene glycol poisoning, into his drink while no one is looking, or so I think. When he comes back, I tell him that I had his drink refilled.

*The Actor*

I eagerly watch him as he takes a small sip, waiting for the poison to cause tissue damage and burn on contact, yet nothing happens. I think to myself, *Maybe I did not put enough in.*

What I did not realize at that time was that the bartender saw me mess with my company's drink, so he swapped the drink with a fresh glass of Ginger Ale when I turned around to greet the lead actor coming back from the restroom.

I greet the man whose part I will be taking soon by asking him a few background questions, like what other pieces of cinema he has been in. The bartender, overhearing our conversation, asks us what we are acting in right now.

I tell him, "My friend here is the lead actor in Macbeth and Julius Caesar, and I am a supporting actor in both."

The bartender congratulates both of us saying, "I think this calls for a few fresh drinks! Is Ginger Ale good for both of you?"

We both nod, and he brings us both glasses of Ginger Ale. We cheers and sip our drinks. Right

*Mirror Image*

---

away my stomach burns, I struggle breathing, and my mouth and face begin to swell.

I never saw it coming, the bartender gave me the poisoned drink. Before I fall to the ground, I glimpse a distorted reflection of mine alongside the smiling face of the actor and bartender.

As the actor went on to play many roles in his life, I wound up as another face in the mirror.

# THE GRAVE DIGGER

## Myself

*Sadness, cold heart, hiding within myself*
*Enveloped in fear, all alone forever*
*Hiding my face. Shock, shame, fear*
*Grief, sorrow, despair*
*Lamenting, regretting everything*
*Walls are barriers blocking my freedom*
*Why am I here? Loneliness, despair*
*Faces show emotions, mine are gone*
*Unseen bruises, victim of abuse. Scared*
*Time stands still. Confined. All alone*
*Dark and light wall, contrast differences*
*Dark floor, light floor, separated me*

*Mirror Image*

---

I reread the poem I'd just written, and can't believe I've come to this horrific point in my life. Yet, here I am.

The jagged path on the floor hinders me as I sit with my back against a cold wall, waiting for my fate to be decided. The room has no windows. I am locked away in a cell that allows the darkness to envelope me.

Life's hard in this darkened cell, and the smile on my face would scare the others that are here, telling then I am far from done. I look in the small mirror in my cell, and what I see is not the same face that I saw years ago. I am older, have more wrinkles, and my face looks beaten to a pulp since the guards show no mercy. No prisoners have any way to contact each other except through the small vents behind our beds. We occasionally use signals and codes to discuss ways to break out of this place and take revenge on the person who is to blame, but the small mirror I have in my room warns me that it may not turn out like we want. But do I really care? I just want to get out of here.

*Mirror Image*

A few years ago, I decided to go to a cemetery to steal bodies that had just been placed into the ground, so I can sell them to medical schools or give them to doctors who can use the organs for people who need them. I thought, for the first time, what I did mattered. I covered up the holes and places the caskets back down six feet to cover my tracks.

It was all going well until someone saw me take the last few bodies from the cemetery and wanted in on my crimes. There was no way I would share my bounty, so I killed him and buried him in one of the empty caskets. When I got caught, I told them I was doing a humanitarian deed to save lives. I guess they disagreed. So, that is how I ended up here.

One day, I managed to create a makeshift knife with one of the plastic forks and the rocks under my bed. We are told to stand far back when the guards bring us our food, but today I have my own plan. The guard is hardly paying attention because he is focusing on the distraction the inmate next to me is making, so I knock him out and grab his keys. I quickly put on his uniform and steal his gun.

I sneak out of the prison to find a driver jumping out of his vehicle to go inside to the prison, probably looking for me. He didn't turn off his vehicle, so I quickly jump in and take off before he gets back.

Where will I go? How will I remain free?

I drive far away from the prison to a motel. Once I enter the motel I see my face plastered on the screen behind the reception man. I quickly leave, telling the man I will be right back, so he does not become suspicious. Luckily, I find a beat-up truck that looks abandoned. I hot wire it and drive away before the man behind the reception desk realizes who I am.

For days, I drive non-stop. I eventually stop to steal a few clothes from some stands outside and continue driving. I find a small, deserted motel to stay in for a few days until I can find a safe place to go.

Across the street is an ATM and a man getting money out, I go over and hit the man over the head, take his big wad of cash, and take his card that needs a pin. I pry the pin out of him and then kill him.

I have no remorse and life goes on, well mine does anyway.

Eventually I secure a job at a construction site hauling heavy loads of lumber and rocks. I soon realize that staying in one place may be a mistake.

There are three other men in the crew, and one keeps on staring at me, so I do what I have to. I eliminate them all.

I travel some more, finding another motel to stay in for a while. When I look at my face in the mirror, it is a combination of all the faces I have killed in the past. I freak out, scared that this will be my new appearance.

The mirror tells me, "If you do not try to undo what you have done, you will be the face you see in the mirror and wind up in a crowded cell surrounded by those you have killed."

I let this pass from my thoughts and think of the positives that have come from my actions. I have saved so many lives, helped those in medical schools with the bodies I donated, and I killed those with cruel intentions.

I become quite tired of driving around, so I go walk around in a park. I notice there is a huge ravine, so I go to check it out. When I look down, I see my dead body staring right at me. *How can that be?* I think. A black shadow of my body rises from the ravine saying, "You have one more chance to change the past in hope to not wind up in this hole in your future. A limp body with a mirror hovering over you. The only thing you will ever see again is yourself dying."

I laugh at the shadow, yet, deep down, I know that I do not want to end up like that. So, I go back to the motel to try and think of a way out of this mess.

I could kill some people and bury them in the empty graves so the families of the dead bodies I have stolen will have a body to come and visit. Or I could make a visit to the medical school to return the bodies. But the bodies are probably gone. I could go to the doctors who took out the organs, but they probably disposed of the bodies, too.

Since none of that will work out, I go with plan B: forget my dead body in the hole and hope for the best.

I lay down in my bed, and as I turn over, my head hits something hard and my body becomes limp. I open my eyes to find myself buried in a grave in a cemetery. The grave is not filled, and I am left facing the sky, but not only the sky, a huge mirror hangs over my body, so I am left to stare at my dying self for the rest of my life.

# BONUS CONTENT

Excerpts from
*Silent Voices*
and
*Faces Behind the Stones*

by Fran Lewis

# LIES

This stone is devoted to me because I broke some serious laws and wound up with a death sentence because I dared to not lie but tell the truth. Lies are what this country that I was born in was founded and made on. Telling the truth, the whole truth, can often hurt someone's feelings, and make them worry when it's not needed. Telling someone they look ugly or need to go on a diet, even if you're just trying to be honest, is the wrong way to go where I come from. But if someone has a fatal illness, is it better to sugarcoat it and not come clean with the entire truth by telling them they have only a few months to live?

The truth is supposed to set you free, but in this case it would not. My name is Don, and all my life I tried to always be honest, truthful, and never tell a lie. But the state I live in as an adult passed a law stating that being too truthful was sinful, and that being brutally honest and telling the truth was punishable. Your sentence would depend on how strong that truth was or how many you told. This is what was decided.

When asked a question, we must think hard before giving a response, as there are people all around that will know we told the truth since we all wear these truth detectors that are part of our everyday wardrobes. Small little wrist bands that have chips and special sensors help the police or anyone you are near know when you have strayed from telling a lie.

Children are great at lying, and love the fact that when they fail all of their subjects in school they can tell their parents they passed with all As or Bs. They bury the real report card and create one on their computers, print it out—since they all have the templates for the cards—and then show their parents how bright and wonderful they are. But some parents dare to question their children when they don't graduate on time. These inventive liars come up with the fact that if they stay one more year, they get college credit and can get into any school with courses under their belt. Of course, their parents believe them, and would never dare think or say the truth: YOU LIED!

Today started out as any day at work. I work for doctors as a medical assistant and do can-do X-rays. To save money, they even sent me to school to learn how to read the X-rays, so they do not need to send them to another radiologist to be read. But remember, lies are the foundation of our world, and telling a patient the truth about their condition is illegal. It works both ways. However, that's not what got me in trouble.

When things started to quiet down at work and I investigated some old cases where a diagnosis was given—and of course it was a total lie—I began wondering just how many people had died because of me, and because the doctors did not tell them the truth about their conditions. Lives were at stake, but it was thought better not to upset people. So, what if they think they are healthy! Who cares?! In reality, something within me felt a certain tinge of guilt, but since it was a law and I knew that somehow, they would find out if I dared to tell the truth, I fudged my statements and made people feel better about themselves or their illnesses.

Sidney was a man of means, and age sixty-five when he came to Dr. N's office for his annual checkup. The usual blood tests were taken, a general exam done, but when the doctor checked his blood pressure, it was off the charts. The patient saw that it said 173/90, but the doctor told him he was having trouble with the blood pressure machine and not to worry about what it registered.

Sidney was overweight and breathing with difficulty, but the doctor discounted that, too, stating that he might just be nervous. Sending him for a chest X-ray and a CAT scan, the doctor could see signs of clots in his lungs, blockages, and other indications that he might need further tests, and should have been referred to a heart

*Lies*

doctor for a follow up. Instead, Dr. N told him to go on a diet, lose weight, walk or join a gym, and not to worry about anything, that his tests had come back with no anomalies, nothing that stuck out as unusual, and said, "See you next year."

I began feeling more pangs of guilt but could not say anything as the doctor was in charge. When Sidney asked for a written report of his test results, I knew this was my chance to help him even if it meant telling the truth. However, the doctor read over the report I prepared, and I knew that I'd missed my chance since he had to sign off on it.

Lying is okay if it doesn't hurt anyone or hinder their lives. Telling a child that they play the piano well even if they do not is that bad, since we hope it won't hurt their feelings or discourage them from trying harder. Lying is okay when you tell a child that he/she will become a singing star and you know they're tone deaf. The child is only five, so no big deal. Right?

Lying is fine when you go into a bank and claim you need a loan because you want to buy a new house for your family, but you want the money for something else. Lying is okay when you can justify the reasons and can live with yourself after you tell the lies: You look amazing. (When the person looks like a fat cow); that dress looks great on you, Mrs. Jones. (It's two sizes too small, but she is smiling as she buys five more and you get a big sale.)

What about the car salesman that sells you a used car that he knows has some mechanical problems? He never tells you about them because he figures by the time they become apparent the car will be yours, and in the fine print it says once it leaves the lot, they are not responsible for anything that goes wrong.

Lies, lies, and liars are what this country is about. Politicians lie all the time and never keep their word or promises. That's how they are programmed to get ahead. Nothing really gets done, but a politician states that he is lowering taxes and providing more money for education and road repairs, while the budget is in trouble

*Lies*

because he bought his wife and children new cars and houses.

So, what happened that I am no longer here? You guessed it! I dared to countermand what Dr. N told Sidney by preparing an unsigned report, telling him the truth about his heart problems, and then went back and mailed reports to three other people that might be alive today if they'd believed what I wrote and what they read.

Living here in this world, those that tell small truths are sentenced to ten days in liar's boot camp to revamp their lying skills and are fined for their transgressions. Those that dare to tell the whole truth and nothing but the truth are subject to severe penalties, as they are tried in a court of law and sworn to tell a lie; but of course, they don't.

Just how does someone know that they told the truth? Somewhere, where you record your daily lies and your thoughts, sometimes people will add another section in their notebook of what really is the truth, hoping no one will care to read it or notice it. They list it as outlandish lies, but when the incidents are compared, and the logs are read by the log overseers each day—and there are many—sometimes they compare notes. And when the truth comes out you are done.

Lies are not so bad if they are not harmful or hateful in context. But when they harm someone, take people's lives by omission because a medical provider does not want the person to unduly worry—that is wrong, and that is the truth, I fear.

Another thing, before I end my tale of pure truth, is that the car salesman sold that car claiming that, even though it was used, it had been tested and test driven for safety precautions. But it was sold in the same condition as when the previous owner brought it in. The result was that the man who bought it was in a serious car accident a few days later because the brakes were worn. He couldn't stop the car and went onto the side of the road, where the entire front end of the vehicle was demolished. He lost a leg and a hand because of the accident.

*Lies*

Had he known the truth he might have thought twice before buying the car, might have had it tested, and might have had repairs done at his cost or the car company's cost, or bought something else. Truths, when it comes to lives, should be told. Truths when it might be hurtful to someone's feelings. So, what if you lie.

*What do you think? Lies vs. Truths: Which would you rather hear?*

My voice is silenced since I was sentenced to the death penalty for making sure that Sidney knew the truth about his diagnosis before he passed on from this world. His family was shocked, and believe it or not, sided with the doctor, claiming that at least he passed peacefully, not knowing the truth and not suffering. His voice is silent, yet I wonder what he would say if he could be heard.

There were so many voices that were silenced. There are many more that will follow. But for right now, you, the reader, will decide if all these people deserved their fates or some might have been victims. I lied and I fudged the truth, and my soul feels so lonely, and the pain that I inflicted on others by lying haunts me even in death. But maybe the truth is that if someone is brave or bold enough to tell those I hurt what they really should know will set my soul free so that I can live in eternity in peace.

# I HATE MYSELF

*Belinda Morris is a depressed and overweight teenager: hear her voice and understand her pain*

Looking at her image in the mirror Belinda realized that what she saw depressed her and she wanted to change it all. How could she turn herself into someone pretty if all she saw was an alter image that reminded her of something she did in the past.

My life as a teen was really so difficult. What did I do to deserve so many tortures? First, being 16 is not easy. Temptations fly in front of your face, and everyone tells me it is up to me to decide whether to succumb to what they refer to as peer pressure, going along with the crowd or heaven help us, think for myself.

*Bonus Content*

Drugs, alcohol and sex are frirst and foremost on the minds of many teens. What some of my friends are into I am not. Many uses recreational drugs, smoke pot and even have an occasional drink. I really don't see the need or the attraction of ruining my lungs and chancing getting a fatal disease, drinking to get liver problems, or having sex and getting a communicable disease: or worse still, pregnant.

But that's just me; and then there is everyone else. I love parties just like the next person, but lately I have been passing on many of them since I am not into a lot of what goes on there. I guess that makes me weird, a freak, or just someone with an independent mind. How strange is that?

Learning to deal with these added pressures makes being a teenager difficult. I personally think they need to write a manual of instructions to help us figure out what we are supposed to be doing opposed to what we are not. Deciding whether to go along with the crowd is an issue I now face. But, even worse is having no one to talk with and share my thoughts, fears and ques-

*I Hate Myself*

tions. You see, the one person I had — my sister Marcia — is gone. I'll tell you about her later.

My mom is great, but you know how old people are. She will discuss certain topics with me but not others. For example: PMS. Well, that is one area I am an expert on and do not need any help to define. Dealing with this wonderful prize makes me wonder what women and girls ever did wrong to deserve this pain, torture, and hormonal roller-coaster that comes with bloat and munchies every month.

Sweets like candy and chocolate and other foods filled with tons of sugar and salt appease me. The result is I'm gaining weight and my stomach looks like a water balloon filled to bursting.

Next, of course, are the wonderful bodily changes that occur. In my case, at age ten I looked like I was 16 or even older because of my overdeveloped chest. Think about going to high school with size 34 DDs poking out in front of you. The stares you get from the boys in your class are just priceless.

Yeah! 34 DDs on a girl who is barely five feet tall and overweight. Growing up happened too fast for me and it wasn't pleasant.

This morning I woke up feeling down. My normally perky mood seems to have disappeared. Why? Let's get to the meat of this story and understand why I, Bertha, am still having trouble socializing. My latest problem is no date for the junior prom.

No date for prom or the party afterwards. How traumatic is that? Pretty darned traumatic. *Is it okay to go alone?* I wonder.

Well, prom night is only three nights away, and I still don't have a date. I've been told it's not wise to go alone. Personally, I really don't care, but since I don't want to put myself in a position I'll be ridiculed more than I already am, I think I'll just pass on the entire thing.

I know many teens like me feel the same way. But, there are a few who have the courage to take a stand against the mean girls who are so popular they can't see anything other than makeup, hairstyles, figures and clothes.

## I Hate Myself

Dating is serious business as far as I'm concerned, as is knowing the right way to act and control yourself. I wish my sister were here, but now she's gone to college, so I'm all alone.

My sister had tons of dates, but I've never even been asked to go to the movies. My mom told both of us we need to go out in groups and never to be alone when on a first date or even a second. We neither one really understood the seriousness of what could happen when you're alone in a car with a boy.

She instructed my sister, who definitely did listen, to make sure she always had her phone charged and ready to go, never accepted an open drink from anyone and definitely never let peer pressure make her do something just to keep a boy in her life or to be part of the group.

So, what am *I* going to do? I have no idea, and as I said, the prom is three days away. I've asked some other kids to weigh in and here is what they have to say on the issue:

Susan: I would never go to a prom by myself. I would be too embarrassed.

*Bonus Content*

---

Joanie: I would go to the prom with a group of girls and we could still have fun dancing and enjoy the food and just being with friends.

Maggie: Never catch me without a date.

Joyce: I would take my brother before going alone, or a cousin that no one knows.

Faith: I would never go alone to a prom. I would rather stay home.

Many girls feel they would be made fun of if they went to a prom or a dance without a date. They never really think about the fact that there might be some guys who just want to hang out and not be bothered by going on an "official" date. They just might go to hang with their friends, and you never know — you just might have some real fun with someone nice.

The only way I could go to the prom would be…well that's not an option anymore because I've decided to put an end to this trauma called life. I put on my prom dress, fix my hair and makeup, play my favorite song and then lie down on my bed and wait until I feel no more pain.

*I Hate Myself*

Instead of enduring more embarrassment, Belinda became the face behind a large pink granite stone. This one has dancing shoes, book covers and some flowers on top. There are some apology notes and cards attached to each side of the stone. Some notes are from her tormentors and others are from her family. It was all too little too late…Pay attention to her story before it happens to someone you love.

## Epilogue

Many young people are self-conscious about how they look and just want to be accepted by the cool or popular crowd. Belinda had a pretty face, but she had a really poor self-image. So, when others commented on her appearance, clothes and such, she would withdraw and feel worthless.

There was no one there to defend her or explain to her that she was fine the way she was. Pressure to have a date for the prom is common and many girls feel ostracized and dejected when they attend these events with a group of friends or even alone instead of with a date.

Belinda took the wrong way out, so heed her story and learn from it. To all those girls that are mean, cruel and help create the problems that caused Belinda to take her own life: read this and think before you act.

# THE CON ARTISTS

Darkness envelopes the next three bodies that are hidden behind stones. These are quite different from the ones in many cemeteries. The surrounding area is desolate, and there are never any visitors here.

On each stone is the face of the person beneath the stone, looking forever as they appeared at their death. Whether they were murdered, beaten, or tortured, their final expressions were photographed, and their faces engraved on each stone, with their exact final expressions of terror.

This is a cemetery no one dares to enter, as some think those beneath the stones rise at night. Each one of these evil coffin dwellers did something so heinous, so horrendous, that they are trapped eternally in this cemetery called the Gravediggers Delight.

A judge will tell the story of these three grave dwellers, who are here because they did something to other people that warranted being placed in this horrific place. Their tortured souls and bodies will rot within the confines of their coffins, which are just wooden boxes nailed shut. Their final repose and their burial were nothing more than the gravediggers' digging holes and literally dropping the coffins in them, and then covering them with sand.

My name is Judge Stanford Brown, and I am your narrator. For most of my life I practiced law, until I was finally appointed to the bench. However, marrying my wife, Denise, I learned that her father was connected to the mob and was a higher up drug lord, which I did not know when I signed the prenup before marrying someone half my age. Learning the ropes about being his son-in-law, it became apparent that when members of his drug team or members of his family came into my court, I had better make sure that they did not get jail time and that bail was set.

Marvin was my accountant, and he dealt with my taxes, books, and more. He was relatively honest until he was not. You'll hear more about this as the story unfolds.

Daniel was the final member of this group. He was our lawyer, and if you think dishonest wait until you learn more about him.

This is their story: The Judge, the Lawyer, and the accountant.

\*\*\*

This cemetery has us backed away in three wooden coffins, nailed shut. I can imagine you are wondering just why we are being treated as if we are undesirables, untouchables, and horrific souls that will be haunted for all eternity. What could each of us have done?

Morris was the accountant for my law firm, and he managed to help me fudge the books so that my partners never knew why we were always in the red. My accounts were in the black, but in foreign banks under an alias. John, the judge, knew of our dealings, since Morris was his lawyer, too, for other enterprises that he was into. For example, when some top mob bosses came up for trial and were sent to his courtroom, for some reason, they never got any real prison time, and some got off with a fine.

John was connected to these people and took bribes, mostly because if he didn't pass the right sentence, they kill his family or some of his friends. They wouldn't hesitate to teach him a lesson about never crossing a mob boss.

The mob boss's son was a captain in the local police force, and his uncle was the chief of police. Possession of drugs, guns, and other small weapons, money laundering, mob kills that would appear to be accidents, and other crimes were just a few that no one could or would be able to prove.

No one ever really knew about our connection until a reporter named Stella overheard something that would take us all down. Just why she was still walking around was beyond all of us, and just how she managed to infiltrate our group is what I will relate next.

Stella was a double agent who appeared to be a reporter, but she was the daughter of the mob boss, and managed to overhear us talking about trying to disconnect ourselves from the mob and attempt to run a legitimate business. Well, not quite legit, but no longer having to pay them protection money, take bribes to fix cases, and, of course, do the once in a while odd jobs that they required in order for us to stay afloat.

\*\*\*

This is John, the judge. Stella came to my courtroom pretending to cover the story of Antonio, accused of killing the butcher on our street. Of course, he claimed it was not him but someone else, but the cameras in the store showed that it was him. Somehow, when the evidence was to be presented in court by the prosecutor, the tapes disappeared from the evidence room, the notes prepared by the arresting detective were not placed in evidence, and the arresting officer went missing.

What happened next was not expected, and the result was that the prosecuting attorney and the defense attorney had to decide whether to proceed with the case or set Antonio free, knowing that he did kill the butcher. Could this somehow be connected to someone on the force? Was there someone that owed Antonio a favor?

Somehow, this required a decision from me, the judge, and I realized that it would place me in an odd position if I let Antonio go. But I had to come up with a way to create some doubt in the jury's mind that this man was guilty.

Lying and cover-ups were becoming the norm in my courtroom. My connection to Antonio and his family was not known. My grandson was married to his granddaughter, making it hard for me to bring the hammer down on him. Antonio was one of the tops in this mob family, involved in murder, money laundering, drug dealing, and funneling weapons of all kinds through different channels to arms dealers throughout the world, and even to young kids on the street who wanted to make a buck selling for them.

Taking my gavel in my hand, I stated that I would allow forty-eight hours for both sides to try and get to the bottom of the missing evidence, and possibly find the missing arresting officer. Did I know where the officer was? Did I know where the evidence went?

Someone decided that they would take all of us down. Stella was dangerous, posing as a reporter for a newspaper but connected to the mob, and after overhearing our conversations, she reported back to the mob head. That's when things began to fall apart.

One of the jury members got sick, or at least said she was ill with stomach pains, and then collapsed in the courtroom, causing us to stop everything and call 9-1-1. She had been planted there to divert everyone's attention, pretending to be sick after purposely eating something she knew would irritate her stomach. Spice gave her heartburn, and she purposely did not take her *Nexium*.

Her chest pains appeared to be real, and her heartburn was over the top, she said. But was she that much in pain? I doubted it, but she accomplished what needed to be done. I had made sure she was on the jury, and that stopped the proceedings so that I could get a handle on what I had to do next.

Court had to be adjourned until we knew what happened to this juror, and an alternate was not in the cards if I wanted the trial to turn out the right way. Hoping that no one else got sick for legitimate reasons, we adjourned for the day, and court would reconvene in the morning at nine promptly.

Things do not always turn out the way you want. Something was wrong with this juror that even she did not know, and the result was she would not be returning any time soon. Now what was I going to do? After all, she was the foreman, and would have been able to sway the jury either to acquit the defendant or to consider a hung jury.

Both attorneys wanted this over with, but no one more than me, so I came up with an idea that I hoped would not backfire. With an alternate juror in place who seemed attracted to me, I insisted on questioning her in my chambers. What transpired I hoped would lead the verdict in the direction that I hoped for.

But something strange happened when I went back on the bench. My coffee cup was on my desk. I got up for ten seconds to use the bathroom to wash my hands, and never thought that anyone would taint my coffee with something that would take me out of commission for good. As the jury was now in place and the trial resumed, I felt pains in my stomach, hot flashes, and then keeled over. The next thing I knew I was being placed on a stretcher, and the EMT looked me straight in the eye and said this was a present from Antonio.

This might be the end of my story, but I am sure there are others that will suffer at the hand of this man because of what he wanted hidden. My voice is silenced; let's hope more will be, too!

# GOING NOWHERE

## Tom McMann's Voice

Tom is the face behind a very large stone at the end of the driveway of this cemetery. The stone is engraved with the word: NOWHERE! This is exactly how the person behind the stone would've described his life. This is Tom's story and it just might send chills down your spine, put fear in your heart and make you glad he is behind the stone and not standing in front of you.

Me belonging to the right fraternity and having the right friends would have made my parents proud. No matter what I did or said they never really gave me any credit. My younger brother by five minutes would have been their whole life, even today, but I had to take drastic measures and find a way to get noticed and rid the world of this perfect person. He was their pride and joy and still is in their minds; a heart surgeon and head of a hospital with a gold-digging wife and three obnoxious kids.

Ted spent his life trying to make my parents proud and make my life miserable. Varsity basketball star, head of the debate team and track star, he could do no wrong and was everyone's choice for class president. I, on the other hand was clever, conniving and definitely much smarter than my brother, but I had no chance.

I graduated and also became a cardiac doctor. My family never really accepted me and my parents never thought I'd amount to anything, even though I'd' become a doctor.

Did I tell you Ted and I were identical twins? Growing up we would switch places and often play tricks on other people. But, as we got older, you could definitely tell us apart. I weighed a lot more than my brother and we wore different styles in clothes. I also had to wear glasses.

It was an odd day when I realized that everything that Ted did was for a reason, and I learned that there was much more behind Ted's financial success when I overheard a phone conversation one day.

## How It All Started

Walking into Ted's house one day I heard him on the phone in the study, whispering so no one would hear the conversation if they passed by. Ted never believed in closing doors and he never knew that I overheard him and another doctor discussing their lucrative side business. I'd suspected something was up, so naturally I was all ears when given the chance to nail him.

It seems my brother was into buying and selling body parts for profit. I won't get into how he managed to get these organs, but let's just say many of his patients never made it to the recovery room. Some made it to the morgue, but not before he removed the organs needed during the operations that should have been successful, with the help of a select staff that knew what he was doing and profited as well.

Just who got these organs and for how much I really didn't hear. I couldn't believe this man who took an oath to help others was playing God with innocent people's lives and had no trouble sleeping at night.

I backed away from the door and reentered, letting him think that I had just arrived. Seeing me he abruptly ended the call and greeted me with his phony smile. So, glad you're here, bro, want a beer? Sure, why not!

We talked for a while and then I knew I had to put my plan in motion. I learned from other people that my dear brother was using sick patients who thought they were terminally ill to be part of his hidden project. He had them sign a paper stating they wanted to donate their organs for research or to another person after they were gone.

What they didn't know was they weren't really terminally ill. Had they gotten a second opinion, they would have learned the truth and survived.

But, my dear brother was the Chief of Cardiac Care, and everyone thought he was a great doctor, so no one thought to question his diagnosis.

After our chat, I claimed that I had some work to do and left. Instead, I went around to the back of the house and down into the basement, where I found the freezer where he kept the evidence that I needed.

For some reason, I can'timagine why, he had the organs brought to his house in coolers, claiming it was beer, ice and other things needed for the parties he frequently threw. No one was the wiser.

His freezer had a huge padlock on it, which would be hard to break. I wasn't worried about that. In the back of the room there was another locked freezer and a safe, which would be easy to open since I knew the combination.

I quickly opened the safe and found the documents I needed. Just as I was turning to leave, I heard footsteps coming down the stairs. Hiding was going to be difficult, but I found a spot in a closet behind one of the freezers.

Three men came into the room, my brother and two mean I assumed were his buyers. I was wrong. One of the men was the police chief! He was in on this scam. I knew he was friends with my brother, but I didn't know the faustian pact they'd made. He obviously kept quiet for a hefty, price, I'm sure.

I'd never seen the other man before, but from what I gathered from their conversation, he needed a heart for his son. I guess someone was going to have to die to make sure that his son lived.

The contract was signed, the price paid and the victim chosen. Poor forty-year-old Irving Schwartz was currently in the hospital because he was experiencing shortness of breath. My brother had apparently kept him there doing unnecessary tests, just so he'd be available when his organs were needed.

Irving was actually suffering from anxiety and not the deadly blot clots he'd been told were the culprits. Again, because my brother was known to be such a good doctor, Irving did just what he

*Mirror Image*

---

was told and agreed to all the tests and staying in the hospital.

But, once Irving had signed all the paperwork for becoming an organ donor, he decided he wanted to leave the hospital the next day. Irving was not a stupid man and, unfortunately for my brother, he didn't take his diagnosis as final.

Before he left the hospital, Irving had made an appointment with another cardiologist. Unbeknownst to him, this doctor was someone who was close to my brother. Well, you can guess what happened next. The second doctor called my brother to find out why his patient was seeking a second opinion.

My brother was furious and called one of his less than law-abiding friends to take care of the problem. Later that day, when he wasn't looking, I grabbed his phone and sent a text to that same criminal friend, making him an offer he couldn't refuse.

The next day, as Irving and and his dedicated cardiologist walked across the hospital parking lot discussing why Irviing didn't need a second opinion, they approached the busy street outside the hospital. As they waited to cross, someone pushed one of the men into oncoming traffic and he was hit by a car.

Poor guy was in bad shape too, but luckily he was near the hospital and was taken directly to the emergency room. Unfortunately, he didn't make it.

Because his records showed he was an organ donor, his heart was quickly removed and the next recipient on the transplant list was called. He received the new heart and his life was saved.

So, who died? Was it Irviing or Ted, my brother? Whose heart has a new home in someone else's body?

I guess you could say I finally put some of my savings toward a good cause. Goodbye forever, Ted.

# Katie's Untimely Death

Driving to the other side of the cemetery, I stopped in front of a stone that was covered with mold and looked quite ignored. I got out of my car, took a cloth and some water and tried to wash off the stains that had marred the words written on this woman's final resting place. As I did this, I heard her voice coming through loud and clear. "Listen to my story. Hear my voice. It is too late for me but maybe you can help someone else."

My name is Katie. I was just 50 years old and could not believe what happened to me. I went to the country club one morning to have lunch with my family and started to feel pains in my chest. I did not say anything to anyone until I was in my room. Max, my husband, was playing cards with some friends and my friend Rosie knocked on my door to see if I was ready to go to lunch.

Feeling a little better, we went into the dining room of the hotel and ordered something light. Never in my wildest dreams would I have thought that I would wind up here in this despicable place six feet underground, stuck in this wooden box with no place to go and definitely no air to breathe.

Sitting at lunch we began to talk about what we would do for the afternoon while Max and Dave, Rosie's husband, were playing cards. All of a sudden, I felt strange. My chest felt like there was a weight on it, and I keeled over.

The next thing I knew I was hooked up to monitors and oxygen, and someone was leaning over me with a sinister smile on her face. "Now to rid the world of you permanently and forever. Katie, you have stood in my way for too long, and now Max will be mine and you will be dust, as they say, when you are finally laid to rest and disintegrate, or whatever happens."

*Bonus Content*

---

I couldn't believe the coldness in her eyes. I had no idea who this person was or why she would want me out of the way — this couldn't be my friend Rosie. I tried talking, but the tube in my throat prevented me from being heard.

I saw a nurse coming into the room and tried to signal her that something was wrong. This person was going to pull the plug on me if she didn't stop her. Instead, the nurse greeted the woman, tried to console her and told her they were doing their best to keep me alive.

When she asked if I was allergic to any meds, the woman failed to tell her I was allergic to sulfa, codeine and penicillin. So, when they added an IV with meds, they didn't consider what the end result would be.

Looking straight into the eyes of this evil and miserable woman who was supposed to be a friend of mine, I realized my only chance was to somehow signal the nurse with my hands or eyes. I even tried to mouth some words around the tube stuck down my throat.

"Katie, I'm going to give you some penicillin to help you fight the infection in your body. I'll also give you some codeine for the pain."

Looking her directly in the eyes, I tried to make her see how afraid I was. I also raised one arm to push her hand away from me and prevent her from injecting the medicine into the IV.

I even tried kicking her, then tried to signal for her to bring me a pen and paper so I could write down what I was trying to tell her. But, the miserable witch sitting at my bedside told her I was just agitated and to give me something to calm me down.

*What am I going to do?* The end was near, but I was not going down alone.

The evil woman stared directly into my eyes and smiled as the nurse gave me the fatal dose that would end my life.

Just then, Max walked in and the nurse told him what she was doing. I couldn't beleive he said nothing. The cold look in his eyes let me know he and my nemisis were in this together.

Chills ran down my spine as tears came streaming down my face. My heart was racing in fear and I knew the end was near for me. My throat felt tight and my mind started to drift away.

I remembered the day I met Max — it was the first time I'd ever seen him. My thoughts drifted back to when we first met. We were so full of life, ambition and hope for our future.

We met because I bumped into him when I was walking out of Macy's. He was tall with dark brown hair and blue eyes that were bluer than the sky. His smile would light up any girl's heart.

Looking straight into his deep blue eyes, I knew it was love at first sight. We introduced ourselves and I apologized for bumping into him. We had a good laugh, and then decided to go around the corner to have some coffee and get to know each other.

Was my untimely death planned all along? Did he and my friend had this in mind from the beginning? Did they just wait until I made a will

## Katie's Untimely Death

after we were married adn then find a way to take me out of the picture?

I was loaded, and I'd left everything to my loving husband in the event of my death. My father was one of the ten richest men in the world and my mom was a famous writer, and they'd left me everything when they died.

I was pretty well known myself. I had my own weekly radio show, I'd written 10 novels, and I was the voice of Emily Sue on a weekly cartoon show.

I really never cared about wealth or fame. I loved my parents and respected them for who they were, and I even loved what I did. So, meeting Max the way I did made me think it was destiny and he loved me for for who I was.

He'd probably done a background check on me before we even met. Now, I was going to die and he was going to get everything.

What I didn't know until recently, was that he was a gambler. He loved the horses, the track, and the casinos, and they loved him too — because he always lost, and lost big.

So, now I'm here, moments from death, in this awful hospital bed and he's got his arm around my "best" friend. They're just sitting there waiting for me to take my last breath so they can go out and spend all my money.

The nurse might have administered the lethal dose and the pain I was feeling was practically gone, but I would manage to inflict one last blow on these two before I left this world.

I put my arms out toward Max, letting him think I wanted to say my last goodbye. So he stood, came to my bedside and bent down He didn't see the sharp object that I had in my left hand. The nurse hadn't completely emptied the syringe filled with the pain medicine because she got called away. She'd left it next to my left arm.

Morphine should do the trick nicely. Max feels tired, nauseous and has a really bad reaction to morphine, poor baby.

He placed his lips close to my right ear and began whispering something I could hardly make out because the drugs were slowing down my thought processes. My throat was closing up

*Katie's Untimely Death*

and I began choking, making the breathing tube constrict my breathing even more. I wanted to rip it out because I knew I could probably breathe on my own but now it was too late.

"Katie, sorry it has to end this way. Some things have to be the way they are and you have been a real albatross around my neck for too long. Rosie and I have been together the whole time, and you were too stupid and naïve to see it.

"I'll enjoy spending all your money, so you just go ahead and go into the great beyond," he said with a gleam in his eye and a vicious smile on his lips.

I lifted my arm with all the strength left in me and stabbed him in the neck. I kept stabbing him, even after the morphine was gone. I wanted him to die, but Rosie stopped me from finishing the job.

I hoped the morphine would do its job and make him sick. But nothing happened. Then, out of the corner of my ele, I saw Linda, my nurse, counting out five one-hundred-dollar bills and smiling. She'd betrayed me too. That was the last thing I saw before closing my eyes one last time.

Katie never made it out of the ICU. She never knew the fate she bestowed on her husband Max. It seems that Rosie and Linda had a plan of their own and the drug Katie injected in Max's neck was way more deadly than morphine.

Goodnight, sweet Katie. .. Rot in hell, Max.

# FRIEND OR FOE?

Driving along, I saw one gravestone all by itself. No one seemed to have come to visit this stone. There were no flowers, the grass was overgrown, and there were cobwebs and weeds all over the place. But, if you listen, you'll hear a voice crying to be heard. That voice belongs to Don Smith.

Don owned a hardware store for many years, always at work by 7 a.m.. to set up the workstations, sweep and make sure the trash was placed on the curb for sanitation to take. Next door to the hardware store was a coffee shop that made the best lattes in the all of the Bronx.

Don loved his coffee and his bran muffins. Every morning like clockwork, he arrived at the coffee shop at 6:30 and had his favorite blend for the day and his muffin. But, today was inventory Friday and Don and his assistant were supposed to be at the shop at 5 a.m. to inventory the boxes delivered the night before.

Don arrived at the same time that a black sedan pulled up in front of the store. Thinking it was Ted, his assistant, he opened the shop, went in and didn't lock the door behind him as he normally did.

I never saw who came into the store that morning. I had my back to the register and I was bent over some boxes with keys, fuses, hammers and other things that I had ordered. Opening the boxes and checking things off of the master list, I never saw the person coming into the store and the next thing I knew I was out cold.

Something sharp and hard hit me over the head, but not before I smelled and recognized the person's cologne and realized who it was. But, it was too late. Why would someone want me out of the way?

*Mirror Image*

Let's go back in time, although I am now six feet underground behind this stone that has turned green with mold, with no one coming to see me except this lone driver. Hear my voice as I tell you my story and maybe you will come and visit me, and I won't be the lonely person behind that last stone in the cemetery.

I was the manager and owner of Hardware City. My wife Eugenia and my daughter Maria always helped me in the store on the weekends when we were the busiest. Ted, my assistant, was quite helpful, but lately he'd been calling in sick, coming in late and just wasn't very dependable.

Last week something strange happened. An unknown caller kept calling at the same time each day, leaving the same message: "I know who you really are and I know what you did."

This message was repeated over and over again until I just stopped answering the phone when this person called. I called the police and had them listen to the tape. After th is, I told my good customers to call me on my cell phone if they needed to order something. This was getting frightening.

That Wednesday I arrived, after getting my coffee and muffin at the shop next door, to see the front door covered in red paint with the following message:

YOU ARE GOING TO DIE! YOU DESERVE
WHATEVER I DO TO YOU!
SIGNED:
YOUR FATE

My hands began to shake and the coffee dropped on the sidewalk. I barely made it inside, where I tried dialing the police; the lines were cut. Using my cell phone, I managed to dial 9-11 and then my wife. I was having trouble breathing and my blood pressure must have shot up way above normal.

When the police arrived I told them what had happened and what was written on the front door. They just stared at me in disbelief. "There is nothing on your front door, Don. You must be seeing things. Also, when we traced the calls on your phone, the only ones that were listed were

*Mirror Image*

your regular customers and your family. The unknown caller must have been another figment of your imagination."

The officer told me not to bother them again, and my wife stood in the background with a strange look on her face. Something weird was happening. I'm not one to imagine things. How could the paint disappear from the front door? Who could have cleaned it up? Who wanted me out of the way and what part did my wife have in all of this?

I sent my wife home and told her to call me when she arrived, but I never heard from her. I tried calling her and got her voicemail. Trying to shake off the events of the day, I opened the store and dealt with all of the customers by myself, since my assistant called in sick once again.

At five, I left to go home. I sensed someone was following me, and I was uneasy to say the least. When I arrived home, Eugenia was making dinner like nothing had happened. So, I asked her why she didn't called me when she got home.

She claimed she called and got my voicemail, which wasn't true.

I ended up thinking I was working too hard or and I decided to put the entire incident aside. I shouldn't have done that.

I bet you're wondering what I could have done to warrant this treatment. As a teenager, I did some things I'm not proud of. I never hurt anyone, hit anyone or stole anything, but I wasn't very nice to some of the kids and would pick on them and call them nasty names. I even tripped the nerdy kids when they were in gym to make them fall off the balance bar or the horse.

One incident does stand out. Morris was walking into the gym one morning with his friend Sam. Morris and Sam, believe it or not, were both 6 feet tall and weighed over 200 pounds at the age of 16. They were mean and would always play dirty tricks on the other kids. I wasn't much better, but the thigns they did could have seriously injured someone, or worse.

Morris and Sam walked over to me and made me an offer I couldn't refuse. They knew I was the one who locked Stan in his locker for an hour because he'd ratted me out to the gym teacher.

They also knew I was the one who put grease all over the captain of the football team's sneakers because he stole my girlfriend. They knew these things, plus some others I don't care to admit.

They explained what they wanted me to do, and said if I didn't go along with their plan they would make sure I paid for all of my misdeeds. I won't tell you what I did but someone did get hurt and the end result was not pretty.

**Present Day**

I am here because someone found out about what I did and threatened to tell. But, it wasn't Morris or Sam, because they're both in jail.

I'm in the hospital in serious condition with a head injury they think will cause me to be paralized for the rest of my life, if I make it at all. Even though I am on life support, I hear everything that's being said.

My wife doesn't seem to be upset by what's happened to me, and my daughter never comes to see me.

Ted has taken over the store and even asked my wife if he can to buy her out. Eugenia knew about my past because I told her everything before we were married over 20 years ago. Eugenia is 46 and is quite stunning. I'm 50 and still in good shape for a man my age. But, lately, she's been hitting the gym and going out with her single friends two or three nights a week.

The doctor just came into the room and told her the police found a hammer the scene and that's what was used to bludgeon me. There was no sign of forced entry and there were no fingerprints because the hammer was wiped clean.

The store's surveillance cameras were disabled and the previous day's tapes were missing. The police didn't really seem concerned about my condition nor did they think they would find the person who did this to me.

I knew who it was, and now I had to find a way to communicate that to someone I trusted. I needed them to pay this person back for me.

Every near-death experience has a short-lived silver lining. Not really, but let's say that somehow a brief miracle occurred as someone walked into the room with the medical staff that was about to remove my life support.

For one brief moment, I opened my eyes and stared into the face of my killer. In that instant, I was able to lift my hand and point a finger at this person. That was all it was but it was enough.

As the nurse was about to put another IV in my arm and shoot me up with morphine to hasten my demise, I did something no one expected. I was going to out my killer from beynond the grave.

I never blackmailed this person and I never would've give them up. The evidence of what they did was in a safety deposit box at my bank. They only way anyone would ever know was when I was dead and gone.

My banker had the only other key and he had instructions to make sure the contents of the box were revealed if I died unexpectedly.

You might wonder why the police didn't follow up on the threats and odd phone calls I reported? Why they never did anything to find out and they never would.

Sometimes, your past becomes your present and things you don't want others to learn about are revealed. Officer Jones was not who he said he was; he was really a hit man for Morris and Sam. He'd been sent to make sure I was silenced. But, I'd have the last word from the grave!.

Made in the USA
Middletown, DE
29 December 2023